Vimal Adiraju

Second Grade Rules!

D0012786

Ready, Freddy! Second Grade Rules!

by ABBY KLEIN

illustrated by
JOHN McKINLEY

Scholastic Inc.

To Dani and Josh — My California babies who love
walking on the beach and searching for sea glass.
Love you always . . .
A.K.

ISBN 978-0-545-69031-7

Text copyright © 2014 by Abby Klein
Illustrations copyright © 2014 by John McKinley
All rights reserved. Published by Scholastic Inc.
SCHOLASTIC and associated logos are trademarks
and/or registered trademarks of Scholastic Inc.

12 11 10 9 8 7 6 5 4 3   15 16 17 18 19/0

Printed in the U.S.A.   40

First printing, September 2014

CHAPTERS

I have a problem.
A really, really big problem.
I am now in second grade,
in a new class with a new
teacher, and my best friend,
Robbie, isn't in my class.

Let me tell you about it.

CHAPTER 1

Missing Robbie

I lay in bed on Monday morning. I could hear my mom yelling from downstairs, "Freddy! Freddy! Let's go! Get a move on!"

"UGGGGHHH!" I groaned.

I didn't want to go to school.

"Freddy! Freddy!" she called again. "You are going to be late!"

I dragged myself out of bed. "Coming, Mom!" I yelled. "Be there in a minute."

I threw on some clothes and walked slowly down to breakfast.

"Well, look who's here," said my dad.

"Ha, ha, ha!" my sister, Suzie, laughed.

"What's so funny?" I snapped.

"You," said Suzie, pointing. "Your hair is a mess. It's sticking out all over. You look like a werewolf."

I tipped my head back and howled, "OOOWWWOOOO!!!"

"And your breath smells like one, too!" said Suzie, waving her hand back and forth in front of her nose. "Peeuuww!"

"Freddy!" said my mom. "Stop howling and come eat."

I plopped myself in my chair and stared at my plate.

"What's wrong?" asked my mom. "Why aren't you eating? I made your favorite, chocolate-chip pancakes."

"I don't want to go to school," I said.

"Why not?" said my mom. "I thought you liked your new teacher, Miss Clark."

"Oh, I like her a lot," I said. "She's really nice."

"So, then, what's the problem?" asked my dad.

"Robbie's not in my class."

"You have other friends in your class," said my mom.

"I know," I said. "But not my *best* friend."

"So what?" said Suzie.

"So what?" I cried. "It's not fair, that's what! You have your best friend in *your* class, so be quiet."

"Freddy," said my dad. "Don't talk to your sister that way."

"Well," I said, "it's *not* fair. Suzie gets to sit next to Kimberly every day."

"But you get to sit next to Robbie on the bus and at lunch, right?" said my mom.

"Yeah, but it's not the same."

"I know it's hard not having Robbie there," said my mom.

"He was in my class in kindergarten and in first grade," I said. "I thought for sure he would be in my class in second grade."

"Sometimes the school likes to mix kids up," said my dad.

"Fine," I said. "Why couldn't they put Max or Chloe in a different class? That would be great!"

"Why don't you try making some new friends?" suggested my dad.

I sighed. "I guess I could."

"What about that new kid?" asked Suzie.

"What new kid?" said my dad.

"There's a new kid in Freddy's class," said Suzie.

"Really?" said my mom. "What's his name?"

"Josh," I told her.

"Where's he from?" asked my dad.

"I'm not sure."

"I wonder why he moved here," Suzie said.

"I think his dad got a new job," I told her.

"I bet he's missing his best friend, too," said my mom.

"Maybe." I shrugged.

"He probably has a best friend at his old school that he misses a lot," said my dad.

"At least you know kids in your class," Suzie pointed out. "He doesn't really know anybody."

I hadn't thought about it like that.

"I think it would be really nice if you tried to make him feel welcome," said my mom.

"Maybe you could ask him to eat lunch with you and Robbie," said Suzie.

"That's a great idea!" said my mom.

"I know," said Suzie, smiling.

"Now, Freddy," said my mom, "you'd better start eating, or you're going to miss the bus."

I reached for the syrup and accidentally knocked over Suzie's glass of milk.

She jumped up out of her chair. "Look what you've done!" shouted Suzie. "I spent a long time picking out this outfit, and now I have to go change my clothes!"

I just stared at her.

"Freddy," said my dad, "don't you have something to say to your sister?"

"Sorry," I mumbled.

"You are so annoying!" Suzie growled as she stomped out of the kitchen to go change her clothes.

"Freddy," said my mom, "stop staring at this river of milk. Go get the sponge and clean up this mess."

"And next time," said my dad, "please ask someone to pass you the syrup instead of reaching for it."

I cleaned up the milk and went back to eating.

"Now you really don't have a lot of time," said my mom. "The bus is going to be here any minute, and you still need to comb your hair."

I started gobbling down huge forkfuls of pancake.

Suzie came back into the kitchen. "That outfit is just as cute as the first one," said my mom.

"Thanks, Mom," said Suzie. Then she turned to me and said, "Not only do you look like a werewolf, but you eat like one, too!"

"I'm just trying to eat fast," I said with a mouthful of pancake.

"EEWWWWW! Keep your mouth closed," said Suzie. "I don't want to see what you're eating! That's disgusting."

"Sorry!" I said as a small piece of pancake fell out of my mouth.

"Gross!" said Suzie.

"Freddy, where are your manners?" said my mom. "You know not to talk with your mouth full."

"Josh isn't going to want to eat lunch with you if you spit food all over him," said Suzie.

"Freddy, run upstairs and brush your teeth and comb your hair," said my mom.

"Yeah," said Suzie. "You don't want to scare kids on the bus. It isn't Halloween yet!"

CHAPTER 2

What Am I?

"I have a fun writing assignment for you all today," said my teacher, Miss Clark.

Miss Clark was new to Lincoln Elementary. She seemed really young, and I thought she was very pretty. She had long, shiny blond hair and bright blue eyes, and she smelled good, too.

"She always has fun things for us to do," Jessie whispered to me.

"I know," I whispered back. "I can't wait to see what it is."

"What is it? What is it?" Chloe squealed, bouncing out of her seat. "I just love writing."

"Sit down, Fancypants," Max grumbled, "and she'll tell us."

"You can't tell me what to do," Chloe said, waving her finger at Max. "You're not the boss of me."

"Chloe and Max, you are not respecting each other," said Miss Clark. "You need to speak more kindly to each other."

"Good luck with that," Jessie whispered.

"Now, Chloe, please sit down, so I can explain the assignment."

Chloe smoothed her dress, fluffed her red curls, and sat down.

"Halloween is coming up," said Miss Clark.

"Yeah, I know!" Max blurted out. "The best holiday ever!"

Miss Clark put her finger to her lips. "This is a listening time, Max."

Max sank back in his chair.

"I thought it would be fun if you all wrote down some clues about what you're going to be for Halloween. Then you'll read them to the class, and we will all try to guess."

Jessie raised her hand, and Miss Clark called on her. "That does sound like fun!" said Jessie. "Can I help?"

"Good, I'm glad you think so," said Miss Clark. "And yes, do you want to help me pass out the writing paper?"

"Why does *she* get to do it?" Chloe whined.

"Because," said Miss Clark, "she was being a respectful student, and she asked."

"Hmmmph," said Chloe, crossing her arms and pouting. "That's not fair."

"It's very fair," said Miss Clark. "I like to reward good behavior."

Jessie passed out the paper, and we all got started. Well, everyone except Max, who just sat at his desk tapping his pencil.

"Stop it! Stop it! Stop it!" yelled Chloe. "I can't think. You are so annoying."

"No, *you* are so annoying," said Max.

"You are!"

"No, you are!"

"All right, enough, you two," said Miss Clark. "One more word out of either of you and you can both go do your work in the principal's office."

They glared at each other and then got to work.

I looked across the room at Josh. *I wonder what he's going to be for Halloween*, I thought. I guessed I would find out soon.

Every year I dress up as a shark, since sharks are my favorite animal. I am obsessed with them! Last year I was a hammerhead shark. This year I planned to be a great white shark, so I had to think of some good clues. I put my pencil up to my mouth and started to chew on the eraser.

"Ewww, what are you doing?" whispered Jessie.

"What do you mean?" I whispered back.

"You're eating the eraser on the pencil!"

"Oh," I laughed. "I didn't even realize I was doing that."

Jessie shook her head. "You're a ding-dong," she said, smiling.

I tapped my pencil on my lips and started writing. Before I knew it, I had written six clues.

Miss Clark rang a little bell. "Okay, everybody, writing time is over. Hand me your

papers, and I'll call you up one at a time to read your clues to the class."

Chloe ran up to the front of the room.

"Yes, Chloe, can I help you?" asked Miss Clark.

"I'm going first," said Chloe.

"No, I'm sorry, you're not," said Miss Clark.

"But I want to," said Chloe.

"You don't get to be first just because you want to," said Miss Clark.

Jessie poked me. "In her world, you do."

"Please sit down and wait for me to call you up," Miss Clark said to Chloe.

Chloe slowly walked back to her seat.

"Let's see," said Miss Clark. "Freddy, why don't you go first."

I walked up to the front of the room, and before I could say anything, Max yelled out, "He's going to be a shark!"

"How do you know that?" asked Miss Clark. "He hasn't even read one clue yet."

"Because he is a shark every year. Boooorrring!" said Max, pretending to yawn.

I started to walk back to my seat.

"Where are you going?" asked Miss Clark.

"Back to my desk."

"Why?"

"Because Max already guessed mine," I said with a big sigh.

"No, he didn't," said Miss Clark.

I looked at her, puzzled.

"He just guessed a shark. He didn't guess what kind. I want to know what kind," said Miss Clark, smiling.

I smiled back and went back to the front of the room. "Okay, here are my clues," I said, and started reading. "This shark can grow to be twenty feet long and weigh four thousand pounds. It is the largest meat-eating shark. It likes to eat seals. It has hundreds of very sharp teeth. It lives in places like Australia, South Africa, and the United States. It is the only shark that can lift its head out of the water to look for food."

"Freddy, are you ready to have people guess?"

"Yes," I said, nodding.

"I know! I know!" Max shouted, waving his hand wildly.

"No calling out, please," said Miss Clark. "I will choose someone with a quiet hand. Jack, you are sitting quietly."

"A whale shark?" guessed Jack.

"Nope," I said.

"Chloe."

"A dolphin shark?"

"A dolphin shark? Ha, ha, ha! That's the funniest thing I've ever heard," said Max. "There is no such thing!"

"Yes, there is, Max. You be quiet!" said Chloe. "It's my turn."

"Freddy? Is that right?" asked Miss Clark.

"Nope," I said. "There is no such thing as a dolphin shark."

"See, I told you," Max said to Chloe.

"If you two cannot behave, you will not have a turn," said Miss Clark. "Josh, do you have a guess?"

"A great white shark?"

"Right!" I said, and smiled. "You got it!"

Josh smiled back.

"Josh, would you like to go next?"

"Sure."

"Oh, wait! Look at the time!" said Miss Clark. "I can't believe it's lunchtime already. We'll have to finish the guessing game after lunch. It will be Josh's turn. I can't wait to hear his clues."

Me either, I thought as I got in line behind him. "Hey, Josh, you want to sit with me and my friend Robbie at lunch?" I asked.

He turned to me and smiled. "Sure," he said.

CHAPTER 3

California Cool

"Hey, what's up?" said Robbie as he sat down next to me at the lunch table. Even though we weren't in the same class anymore, Robbie and I still ate lunch together every day.

"Not much," I said.

"Who's sitting next to you?" Robbie whispered.

"Robbie, this is Josh," I said. "I asked him if he wanted to eat lunch with us today."

"That's cool," said Robbie. He turned to Josh. "Are you in Freddy's class?"

"Yeah," said Josh.

"Is this your first year at this school?"

"Yep."

"Where are you from?" asked Robbie.

"My family just moved here from California," said Josh.

"Wow! California!" said Robbie. "That's far away."

Josh nodded.

"I always wanted to go to California," said Robbie, "and go to Disneyland."

"Disneyland! I want to go to Disneyland," said Max as he tried to squeeze himself in between Josh and me.

"Go away!" I mumbled.

Max grabbed my shirt. "What did you say, Sharkbreath?"

I gulped. "Nothing," I whispered.

"Come on, Freddy," said Jessie, sitting down on the other side of our table. "Tell Max what you really said."

"Yeah, tell me what you really said," Max repeated, tightening his grip on my shirt.

I gulped again. I couldn't get the words to come out of my mouth.

"He said, 'Go away!'" said Jessie.

"Is that what you said?" Max asked me.

I looked at Max, then at Jessie, and then back at Max. I nodded my head.

"Make me!" said Max.

"I'll make you," said Jessie as she started to stand up and walk around the table.

Max began to back away.

"That's right," said Jessie. "Go find another place to sit."

Max glared at her, turned, and walked away.

"She's really brave," Josh whispered to me.

"I know," I said. "She's the only one brave enough to stand up to Max. He used to be the biggest bully in the whole first grade, and now he's the biggest bully in the whole second grade!"

"That was amazing," Josh said to Jessie as she sat back down.

"Thanks," said Jessie, smiling. "Max just thinks he's all that, but he really isn't."

Josh laughed.

"So, Josh," said Robbie, "have *you* ever been to Disneyland?"

"Oh yeah. Lots of times."

"Really?" I said. "You are so lucky!"

"So, why did you move here from California?" asked Robbie.

"My dad got a new job."

"Do you like it here?" asked Jessie.

"It's okay," said Josh, "but I miss the ocean."

"Did you live near the ocean?" I asked.

"Yeah, I could walk to the beach from my house," he said, nodding.

"No way!" I said.

"That is so cool," said Robbie. "Have you ever been surfing?"

"I love to surf," said Josh. "My dad taught me how. We would go almost every weekend."

"I am so jealous," I said. "That sounds like so much fun!"

"It is," said Josh.

"You even look like a surfer," said Robbie.

Josh had on a shirt with a surfboard on it, shorts that looked like a swimsuit, and flip-flops.

"You know, you won't be able to dress like that for very much longer," said Robbie. "It gets really cold here in the winter."

"I know," said Josh. "That's a bummer."

"Not really," I said. "There are lots of fun things to do in the snow. Maybe you can even

learn to snowboard. That's kind of like surfing on snow!"

"That sounds awesome!" said Josh. "Do you snowboard, Freddy?"

I shook my head. "Nope. I wish I did. But I love to go sledding."

"I've never been sledding before," said Josh.

"Never?" said Jessie.

Josh shook his head. "There wasn't any snow where I lived."

"Then you are in for some fun," I told him.

"As soon as there's enough snow on the ground, we'll take you sledding," said Jessie. "Just be ready to go fast!"

"I love fast things," said Josh. "The faster the better!"

"Hey, Josh," said Robbie, "Halloween is only a couple days away. Do you have someone to go trick-or-treating with?"

Josh shook his head.

"Do you want to go trick-or-treating with me and Freddy?"

"Really?" said Josh. "That would be awesome!"

"Yeah, that would be awesome," I agreed. "What are you going to be?"

Josh laughed. "I was actually thinking of dressing up as a surfer."

"It looks like you already have your costume," I said.

"I figured I could wear this stuff," Josh said, pointing to himself, "and bring a little mini surfboard made out of cardboard."

"Great idea!" said Jessie.

"And I have an even better idea," said Robbie. "Since Freddy is going to dress up as a great white shark, and the two of you are going to go together, you could make it look like your surfboard has a bite taken out of it!"

"Ha, ha, ha!" I said. "That's so funny."

"Yeah, that's really funny," said Josh.

"You are so smart, Robbie," said Jessie. "I love that idea!"

"That would be perfect," I said. "The great white shark and the surfer."

We all high-fived each other.

"I'm glad Freddy asked you to eat lunch with him today," said Robbie.

"Yeah, me, too," said Josh, smiling. "Me, too."

CHAPTER 4

The New Kid

I was excited to tell my whole family all about my trick-or-treating plan with Josh. I decided to wait until my dad got home from work.

"Freddy, time for dinner!" my mom called.

I raced down the stairs and skidded into the kitchen, almost knocking into the table. I caught myself just in time.

"Whoa! Careful there, Speed Racer," said my dad.

"Yeah, watch it," said Suzie. "You almost tipped

over my glass of water. I already had to change my clothes once today because of you!"

"This speediness is a little different than your snail's pace this morning," said my mom. "I'm glad to see you more excited."

"Oh, I am excited!" I said.

"Is it because I made one of your favorites for dinner?" asked my mom. "I was trying to cheer you up."

"Thanks, Mom, I do love spaghetti," I said, patting my stomach, "but that's not why I am so excited."

"Then why don't you sit down and tell us why," said my dad.

I jumped into my chair, shoved a forkful of spaghetti into my mouth, and started to talk. "So —"

"Hold on there just a minute," said my dad. "Why don't you finish that mouthful first, and then tell us what you have to say."

I chewed quickly.

"Freddy, slow down. You're going to choke!" said my mom.

I swallowed the rest of that bite. "Guess what," I said.

"You're a weirdo?" said Suzie.

"Ha-ha! Very funny," I said. "No, that's not what."

"Tell us," said my mom.

"I had lunch with Josh today," I said.

"Is he that new kid you were talking about this morning?" asked my dad.

"Yep!" I said, slurping up another big forkful of spaghetti.

"Eeewwww! Gross!" said Suzie. "That is a disgusting sound. Can't you eat like a normal person instead of a pig?"

I turned to Suzie. "I am not a pig!" I said, and a little bit of spaghetti sauce came flying out of my mouth.

"Hey, Pig, say it, don't spray it!" said Suzie.

"Don't call your brother a pig," said my mom.

"Well, he sure eats like one," said Suzie.

"You're right that he has to work on his table manners, but I don't like you calling each other names. Freddy, no more talking with your mouth full!"

"Yes, Mom," I said.

"You can finish your story when you're done chewing."

"Did you find out where Josh is from?" asked my dad.

I nodded. "You won't believe it!" I said. "He moved here all the way from California!"

"California!" said my mom. "That's a big move."

"Does he like it here?" asked my dad.

"I guess so," I said, "but he really misses the beach."

"Did he live near the beach in California?" Suzie asked.

"Yeah, he said he could walk to the beach from his house."

"That must be nice," said my mom. "The beaches in California are beautiful."

"Have you ever been there, Mom?" Suzie asked.

"No, but I've seen pictures, and I've always wanted to go."

"And Josh even knows how to surf!" I said.

"He does?" said my dad. "That's not easy to do."

"Really?" said Suzie. "That's pretty cool."

"I know!" I said. "I think it's super cool! He said his dad would take him almost every weekend."

"I'm so glad you asked him to eat lunch with you," said my mom. "That was a kind thing to do. He seems like a really nice boy."

"He is!" I said.

"And he was probably feeling a little lonely at this new school," said my dad. "Maybe missing his friends from California."

"Guess what else?" I asked everyone.

"You're a dork?" said Suzie.

I glared at her, then turned back to my parents. "I invited him to go trick-or-treating with Robbie and me."

"Really?" said my mom. "I bet that made him happy."

"What is he going to go as?" asked my dad.

I laughed. "A surfer! He's just going to wear his regular clothes and carry a small cardboard surfboard."

"I like that idea," said my mom. "That's a pretty easy costume."

"Why don't you do something easy like that some time," said Suzie, "instead of making Mom spend hours and hours making you a costume?"

"Mom makes the best costumes ever!" I said. "Besides, the Halloween store never has any shark costumes."

"You know, you don't have to be a shark every year," said Suzie.

"Yes, I do," I said.

"You could be something else, like a zombie or Frankenstein," she insisted. "They have those costumes at the Halloween store."

"But sharks are my favorite thing in the whole wide world!"

"I know," said Suzie. "Everybody knows.

It's hard to miss. You have shark shirts, and shark sheets, and shark pajamas, and a lucky shark's tooth, and —"

"I don't mind making Freddy's costumes. I like to sew," said my mom. "It's kind of fun designing a new costume every year."

"What kind of shark did you go as last year?" my dad asked.

"Don't you remember?" I said. "A hammerhead!"

"Oh, right. Right," said my dad. "How could I forget? It took your mother a long time to get the head just the way you wanted it."

"Is my costume for this year almost done, Mom?"

"I still need to do a little more work on it," said my mom. "Maybe after I clean up the dinner dishes, you can try it on, Freddy, and I can measure it some more."

"Sure!" I said. "It's going to be so cool! And Josh is going to make it even cooler."

"Josh?" said Suzie. "What does he have to do with it?"

"Robbie had a great idea today at lunch. He said that since Josh and I are going to go trick-or-treating together, he should make it look like his surfboard has a bite taken out of it!"

"What a cute idea!" said my mom.

"Very clever," said my dad.

"Robbie said that great whites don't mean to eat surfers. It's just that when people lie on their surfboards, they look just like the seals that great whites eat."

"That sounds like something Robbie, the science genius, would say," said Suzie.

"Yes, it does," my dad said with a laugh. "Yes, it does."

I sprang out of my chair. "Trick-or-treating is going to be so much fun this year," I said, jumping around. "I can't wait!"

"Well, you're going to have to wait a little longer," said my mom. "Why don't you swim on upstairs, Mr. Great White, and take a shower. Your mouth is covered in spaghetti sauce, and I think you might even have some in your hair!"

I pretended to swim out of the kitchen and up the stairs.

CHAPTER 5

Rubber Spider

The next morning I jumped out of bed and ran to the bathroom, but it was locked. I banged on the door. "Hey! Hey! Open this door!" I yelled.

"Go away, Hammerhead!" Suzie yelled back.

"I need to get in there to look for something."

"Too bad. You're just going to have to wait," said Suzie.

"I can't wait. I need to get in there right now!"

Suzie didn't answer, and she didn't open the door, so I jiggled the handle. "Open up!"

"No!"

"I guess I'll just have to look for it in *your* room," I said through the door.

Just then, the door flew open. "I don't think so!" Suzie said. "You are not allowed in my room."

I ducked into the bathroom.

"Why, you little . . ." Suzie sputtered. "Get out! Get out!"

I ignored her and started throwing clothes out of the hamper.

"Hey, watch it!" said Suzie. "You almost threw my T-shirt in the toilet! What are you doing?"

"I told you, I'm looking for something."

"What?"

"That rubber spider I got at the Halloween store the other day."

"Why do you need that?"

"I just need it for school."

"Oh really?" said Suzie, smiling. "There are

no toys allowed at school. Maybe I should tell Mom that you're up to something."

I stared at her. "Please don't tell Mom," I said.

"What's it worth to you?" asked Suzie, holding up her pinkie for a pinkie swear.

"Ummm, ummm."

"I don't have all day," said Suzie.

"Okay. Okay. How about three pieces of my Halloween candy?"

"Three pieces? Are you kidding?" said Suzie. "How about six, and I get to choose them?"

"Six?!"

"Take it or leave it."

"Fine, six," I said as we locked pinkies.

"I think you left that spider in the playroom the other day when you and Robbie were playing in there," said Suzie.

"Thanks," I said as I started to run down the stairs to get it.

"You might want to put some clothes on!" Suzie yelled after me. "It's not a good idea to go to school in your pajamas!"

When I got on the bus, I sat down next to Robbie. He always saved that spot for me.

"What's up?" asked Robbie.

"I have a trick I want to play on Chloe today," I whispered, "but since you're not in my class this year, you can't help me with it."

"I really wish we were in the same class," said Robbie.

"Me, too," I said. "It really stinks!"

"Maybe Josh can help you," Robbie said.

"That's a good idea," I said.

Just then the bus stopped at the next pickup, and Josh got on.

"Hey, Josh, come sit over here," I said pointing to the seat right across the aisle from me.

"Hey, Freddy," said Josh as he sat down. "How's it hangin'?"

"Hangin'?" I said.

Josh laughed. "That means, how are you? What's happening?"

"Oh!" I said, laughing. "That must be what they say in California! Everything's great." I leaned closer to him and whispered, "Do you want to help me play a trick on Chloe?"

Josh nodded. "Yeah, she's so annoying!"

"Tell me about it!" I said. "She has been in my class since kindergarten, and I think she gets even more annoying every year!"

"That's the only good thing about not being in your class this year," Robbie said, laughing.

"So, what's the trick?" asked Josh.

"Well," I said, "she's really afraid of creepy-crawly things."

"I bet," said Josh.

I pulled the rubber spider out of my backpack.

"That is so cool," said Josh. "Where did you get it?"

Max's head suddenly appeared over our seat. I quickly hid the spider behind my back. "Get what?" he demanded.

"Nothing," I mumbled.

"What's behind your back?" said Max.

"Nothing," I mumbled again.

"You'd better show me, or else . . ."

"Or else what?" Josh said.

"Ummm, ummm," Max stammered. I think he was just as surprised as I was that Josh wasn't afraid of him.

"Sit down and leave us alone," said Josh. "Mind your own business."

Max stared at him for a minute and then sat down in his seat.

I smiled. "Thanks, Josh."

"No problem," he said. "He just seems scary, but he really isn't."

Robbie leaned over and gave Josh a high five. "Way to go. That was awesome!"

Josh smiled and shrugged his shoulders. "No big deal," he said. "So, Freddy, what's your idea?"

I pulled the spider out from behind my back. "I will hide this spider in Chloe's cubby when we get to school this morning, and then 'accidentally' knock her sweater on the floor. You'll tell her that her sweater fell out of her cubby, and she'll go running to pick it up and put it back in because she hates having her things on the floor. She thinks it's dirty and disgusting."

"Of course she does," said Josh. "She thinks everything is full of germs."

"Then when she goes to put her sweater away, she'll see the spider and freak out!"

"Oh, she'll freak out, all right!" Robbie said.

"So, what do you think?" I asked Josh. "Robbie usually helps me with these little tricks, but he can't this year."

"I think it's hilarious! Of course I'll help you," Josh said.

"I just wish I was there to see it," said Robbie.

"Oh, don't worry, I bet you'll be able to hear her screams all the way down the hall," I said.

"I bet I will," Robbie said, laughing. "I bet I will."

CHAPTER 6

AAAAHHHHHHHH!!!!!

The bus pulled up in front of school, and I stuffed the rubber spider into my pocket.

"Good luck!" Robbie whispered as we got off the bus. "I can't wait to hear all about it."

"Meet me by the big tree at recess," I said, "and I'll tell you the whole story. Bye!"

"Bye!" shouted Robbie as he ran off to his classroom.

"This trick is going to be great!" Josh said, patting me on the back.

"I know," I said, smiling at him. "Really great!"

"What's really great?" asked Miss Clark when we walked into the room.

Josh froze and looked at me.

"Ummm, ummm," I said. I didn't know Miss Clark had heard us talking. "The day . . . today . . . today is going to be really great!"

"I'm glad to hear that," said Miss Clark. "Do you have something special planned?"

I nodded my head. "Yes, I do. Something really special," I said, gently patting my pocket.

"Well, that's wonderful," said Miss Clark. "I'm happy for you. Why don't you go put your things away and get yourself ready, Freddy."

"Okay, Miss Clark. I will." I walked over to my coat hook and cubby.

"Whew! That was a close one," Josh whispered.

I nodded. "A little too close, but I don't think she heard anything."

I hung up my coat and started to empty my backpack.

Chloe came bounding into the room. "Good morning, Miss Clark."

"Good morning, Chloe."

Chloe waved her hand in Miss Clark's face. "Look, Miss Clark! Look at my nails. Aren't they so cute?"

"She always thinks she's *so* cute," said Jessie, rolling her eyes.

"Stop waving your hand so I can see," said Miss Clark. "Oh, look at that. Your nails have little pumpkins on them."

"Who else wants to see?" said Chloe, waving her hands in the air.

No one answered.

"Chloe, you need to put your things away, so we can get started," said Miss Clark. "You can show your friends your nails later."

"Or maybe never," Jessie whispered to me.

I laughed.

Chloe came over to put her things away. She carefully hung up her coat. Then she unzipped

her backpack, pulled out her lunch box, and opened it to inspect what was inside. "Oh, look, my mom packed me finger sandwiches for lunch today," she said.

"EEEWWWW! Finger sandwiches," said Max. "Who wants to eat sandwiches with fingers in them!"

"They don't have fingers in them," said Chloe. "They are called finger sandwiches because they are so tiny you can hold them with just two fingers. Fancy ladies eat them at tea parties."

"Boy, she is taking forever!" said Josh.

"She always does," I whispered. "If she doesn't hurry up, I won't have time to put the spider in her cubby."

"Hey, Chloe, hurry up!" said Max. "You're in my way. I can't put my things in my cubby."

"You'll just have to wait," said Chloe. "I'm not done yet."

"Well, I don't have all day, Fancypants," said Max. "Now, move it!" He gave Chloe a big shove, and she fell on the floor. The stuff in her lunch box went flying everywhere.

"Miss Clark! Miss Clark!" Chloe wailed. "Max pushed me."

"I did not!" yelled Max.

"Yes, you did!"

"No, I didn't. Besides, you were in my way."

"If someone is in your way, Max, then you need to say 'excuse me,'" said Miss Clark. "You just can't push them. Now, tell Chloe you're sorry," she said as she helped Chloe up.

"Sorry!" Max barked.

"Max," said Miss Clark, "you need to say it in a friendly voice."

"Sorry," Max mumbled, looking at the ground.

"Max, look at Chloe and tell her you're sorry."

Max glanced at Chloe and quickly said, "I'm sorry."

Miss Clark helped Chloe get her lunch back in her lunch box. "Now, boys and girls, we really need to finish putting our things away. It's time to get started."

Chloe took off her pink fluffy sweater, folded it neatly, and laid it carefully in her cubby. Then she went to sit down at her desk.

Josh went to sit down, too.

I looked around to make sure that no one was watching me. I secretly pulled the rubber spider out of my pocket, put it in Chloe's cubby, and knocked her sweater on the floor. As I walked over to my desk to sit down, I patted Josh on the back.

"Hey, Chloe," said Josh.

"What?"

"Is that your sweater on the floor?"

"No, it can't be," said Chloe. "I folded my sweater up very neatly and put it in my cubby. It must be someone else's sweater."

"But isn't your sweater pink?" asked Josh.

"Yes," said Chloe. "Pink and fluffy."

"Then it's yours," Josh said, pointing. "Look over there."

Chloe turned her head to look, and then she bolted out of her chair. "Oh no! Oh no! That is my brand-new sweater from Paris. My nana just went on a trip to France and brought it back for me." She picked up her sweater and brushed it off.

"Chloe," said Miss Clark, "please put your sweater away quickly and come sit back down."

Chloe took a step toward her cubby.

I looked at Josh, and Josh looked at me. We smiled.

I mouthed the words, "One, two, three . . ."

"AAAAHHHHHHHH!" Chloe screamed.

I was sure Robbie could hear it all the way down in his classroom.

"Help! Help! A spider! A spider!" Chloe shouted, and she jumped up on a chair. "There's a spider in my cubby! There's a spider in my cubby! Get it out! Get it out!"

"You are such a baby," said Max.

Chloe jumped down off the chair and started running around the room, waving her arms and screaming, "AAAAHHHHHHHHH!"

"Chloe, calm down. Spiders won't hurt you," said Miss Clark. "I'll catch it and put it outside."

Miss Clark got a jar and went over to Chloe's cubby to catch the spider, but when she got there, she started laughing.

"What's so funny?" said Chloe.

Miss Clark picked up the rubber spider. "It's not real," she said. "It's just a toy. I guess someone was playing a practical joke on you."

"Well, I don't think that's very funny," said Chloe.

"Ha, ha, ha! I do," said Max. "I think it's really funny. I wish I had thought of that."

When Miss Clark turned around to put the spider on her desk, I gave Josh a thumbs-up. "Good one," I mouthed.

Josh smiled and gave me two thumbs up.

CHAPTER 7

My Bodyguard

"So, how did it go?" Robbie asked when we saw him at recess.

"It was awesome!" said Josh.

"Yeah, it was great!" I said. "I really wish you had been there to see it, Robbie."

"She was screaming her head off," said Josh. "She even jumped up on a chair."

"Couldn't you hear her in your classroom?" I asked.

"They probably heard it all the way in the office," Josh said, laughing.

"Did Miss Clark know who did it?" asked Robbie.

"Nope. She had no clue," I said, smiling.

"She didn't even really get mad," said Josh. "She just told Chloe that someone was playing a trick on her."

"Wow! That's pretty cool," said Robbie.

"I know," I said. "Really cool."

"I wish I was in Miss Clark's class," said Robbie. "You guys are so lucky you got the new teacher. She seems so nice."

"She's super nice," I said.

Just then Max snuck up on me from behind. "Boo!" he said.

I jumped about three feet in the air.

"Ha, ha, ha!" Max laughed. "You are such a fraidy-cat, Freddy."

I tried to ignore him.

"So, who is super nice?" Max asked. "You just said, 'she's super nice.' Who is 'she'? Your girlfriend?"

"I don't have a girlfriend," I said.

Then Max started singing, "Freddy and Jessie sitting in a tree. K-I-S-S-I-N-G."

"Stop it, Max," I said.

But Max kept on singing. "First comes love, then comes —"

Josh got right in Max's face. "Freddy said 'stop it,' so I think you'd better stop," he said.

"Oh really?" said Max.

"Really," said Josh.

Robbie looked at me, and I looked at Robbie. We both could not believe our eyes.

Josh did not budge. He just stared at Max.

I think Max realized that Josh was not going to back down. "Oh, whatever," said Max. "See you babies later." And he walked away.

"You are really brave," said Robbie.

"Or really crazy," I said, laughing. "I can't believe that you aren't afraid of the biggest bully in the whole second grade."

"Like Jessie said — he wants you to think he's mean and tough, but he really isn't," Josh said.

"Well, *I'm* scared of him," I said.

"He knows that," said Josh. "That's why he picks on you."

"Really?" I said.

"Yep," said Josh. "That's why he never picks on Jessie. She'll stand up to him."

"Jessie is like my bodyguard. Do you want to be my bodyguard, too?" I asked Josh.

"Sure!" he said, laughing.

"Me, too!" said Robbie. "You can protect me, too!"

"I'll protect you both from the Big Bad Wolf," said Josh.

We gave each other high fives.

"Halloween is only two days away," Robbie

said. "We'd better make a plan for trick-or-treating."

"We could all meet at my house," I said.

"My parents have to take my little sister, Dani, trick-or-treating," said Josh, "so if I could go with your family, that would be awesome!"

"Of course you can," I said. "I already talked to them about it, and they thought it was a great idea."

"And Freddy's mom makes the best caramel apples," said Robbie. "Wait until you taste them!"

"Yum! I love caramel apples," said Josh.

"There's only one rule," said Robbie. "You have to eat them on the front porch."

"The front porch? Why is that?" asked Josh.

"Because Freddy's mom is a neat freak," said Robbie. "She doesn't want sticky fingers touching everything."

"Ha!" said Josh. "She'd better not come to my house."

"Why not?" I said.

"Because my mom is just the opposite. We can eat anything, anywhere."

"You can take food up to your room?" I asked.

Josh nodded. "I eat ice cream up there every night, and my dog, Jasper, licks the bowl."

"Lucky!" I said. "I want a dog so badly, but my mom won't let me get one. She thinks they're too smelly and dirty."

"You'll just have to come over to my house and play with mine," said Josh. "And if you come for a sleepover, Jasper might sleep with you."

"Then we'll have to do a sleepover soon," I said.

"Hey, guys," said Robbie, "remember, we're talking about trick-or-treating."

We laughed. "Sorry, Robbie," I said. "You know I just love dogs."

"Are there any cool haunted houses on your block?" Josh asked.

"Oh, there is one that's really awesome," said Robbie.

"What's so cool about it?"

"It's really dark and creepy, and things jump out at you," said Robbie.

"Wow!" said Josh. "We have to go to that one for sure. Right, Freddy?"

"Ummm, ummm . . ." I stammered.

"Freddy is kind of afraid of haunted houses," said Robbie.

"Really?" said Josh.

I didn't want Josh to think I was a baby, so I said, "Well, I, uh, used to be afraid, but I'm not anymore now that I'm in second grade."

Robbie stared at me. "Are you sure?" he said.

I nodded.

"Great! Then we'll definitely go to that one," said Josh.

I swallowed hard. "Yeah, for sure," I said, and gulped again. "Wouldn't want to miss it."

"This is going to be the best Halloween ever!" said Josh. "I thought it was going to be the worst because I didn't know anybody here, but now that I met you and Robbie, I think it's going to be so much fun."

"I know," I said. "I can't wait."

"Me, either," said Robbie. "Yummy candy, here I come!"

CHAPTER 8

Trick-or-Treat

"It's Halloween! It's Halloween! It's Halloween!" I sang as I jumped around the kitchen.

"Freddy, calm down," said my mom.

"But I'm so excited!" I said.

"I know you're excited, but you're going to rip your costume jumping around like that."

"I can't wait for Robbie and Josh to get here."

Just then, the doorbell rang.

"That must be them now," said my mom.

"Mr. Great White, why don't you swim on over to the door and answer it."

I raced into the other room and threw open the door.

"Hi, Freddy," they said.

"Hey, guys. Come on in."

"This is going to be great!" said Josh.

"I'm going to fill up my whole bag with candy," said Robbie. "I want to get even more than last year."

"Yeah, I'm going to fill my bag to the top!" said Josh.

"You must be Josh," my dad said as he walked into the room.

"Yes, I am."

"Nice to meet you, Josh," said my mom.

"Nice to meet you, too. Thank you so much for letting me come trick-or-treating with you."

"No problem," said my dad. "I'm glad Freddy invited you."

"Let's go! Let's go! Let's go!" I shouted. "We have a lot of houses to get to!"

The three of us took off running.

"Don't go too far, boys," my dad called after us. "We need to be able to see you."

"All right, Dad," I yelled over my shoulder.

"Let's go to Mrs. Golden's house first," said Robbie.

"Good idea," I said. "She always has the best candy."

We ran up her steps and rang the doorbell. "Arf! Arf!" we heard from inside the house.

"That's her dog, Baxter," I said to Josh. "Wait until you see him. He's so cute."

Mrs. Golden opened the door.

"Arf! Arf!" Baxter barked again, and came running out dressed as a pirate.

I reached out to pet him. "Hey, Baxter," I said. "Great costume."

He wagged his tail.

"Hello, boys," said Mrs. Golden. "I'm so glad to see you."

"Hi, Mrs. Golden," Robbie and I said.

"Freddy, do you have a new friend?" she asked.

"Yes, this is Josh. He moved here all the way from California!"

"California! Wow! That's a big move. Nice to meet you, Josh."

"Nice to meet you, too."

"Well, Josh, you couldn't have picked nicer friends than Robbie and Freddy."

Baxter barked and wagged his tail some more.

"You see. Even Baxter agrees," said Mrs. Golden.

"Did Baxter eat any pumpkins this year?" I asked.

"He eats pumpkins?" asked Josh.

"He did last year," I said, laughing. "He took it right off my porch!"

"Oh, I almost forgot about that," said Mrs. Golden. "Baxter is a bit crazy. He will eat just about anything! Luckily, he didn't eat the Halloween candy, so I have plenty to give to you. What would you like?" she asked, holding out a big bowl full of candy.

"I'll have a Reese's Peanut Butter Cup," said Robbie.

"I'll take M&M'S," I said.

"I'll have gummy bears," said Josh.

We dropped our candy in our bags.

"Thanks, Mrs. Golden," I said.

"You boys have a great night!"

Baxter barked. "Arf! Arf!"

"Bye, Baxter. You have fun tonight, too," I said. "Just don't eat any candy."

We jumped down her steps, and I started to run past the next house.

"Hey, Freddy, wait," said Josh. "Don't you want to go in here?"

"Go in where?"

"This house here," Josh said, pointing. "You almost ran right past it. This house looks awesome."

"This is the haunted house I was telling you about," said Robbie. "It's really cool."

"Let's go in."

I stood there, frozen.

"What's wrong, Freddy?" asked Robbie. "Did you change your mind? Do you just want to wait out here for me and Josh?"

"Ummm . . . ummm . . . I . . . ummm."

"Come on, Freddy. Come with me," said Josh. "Remember? I'm your bodyguard."

You are in second grade now. You can do this, I said to myself.

"Okay, yeah, let's go," I said.

"Are you sure?" asked Robbie.

"I'm sure," I said.

"Just stay right next to me," said Josh.

I took a deep breath, and we went in. It was pitch-black. My heart was pounding.

"Remember," said Josh, "it's all just pretend."

Before I knew it, our trip through the haunted house was over.

"You were right, Robbie," said Josh. "That was one of the best haunted houses I've ever been in!"

"I just love when people jump out at you in the dark," said Robbie.

"So, Freddy, what did you think? Were you scared?" asked Josh.

I smiled. "Not with you guys by my side," I said. "I actually thought it was pretty cool."

"We'd better get going," said Robbie. "We have a lot of trick-or-treating to do if we're going to fill our bags to the top tonight!"

Then the three of us took off running, singing, "Trick-or-treat. Smell my feet. Give me something good to eat!"

Happy Halloween!

Freddy's Fun Pages

GREAT WHITE SHARK QUIZ

Are you a great white shark expert like Freddy? Take this quiz and find out!

1. What is a baby great white called?

2. Adult great whites mostly eat what?

3. How fast can an adult great white swim?

4. A full-grown great white can weigh up to how many pounds?

5. How long is an adult great white?

Answers:
1. a pup
2. seals and sea lions
3. up to 40 mph
4. 4,000 pounds
5. 20 feet long

GREAT WHITE
SHARK TEETH

Make this delicious and scary treat for your next Halloween party. It's one of Freddy's favorites!

INGREDIENTS:

One Red Apple
Peanut Butter or Marshmallow Spread
Candy Corn

DIRECTIONS:

1. Cut the apple into eight slices.

2. Turn one slice on its side and spread peanut butter on the white part of the apple slice.

3. Turn another slice on its side and place it on top of the peanut butter to finish the mouth.

4. Put a row of candy corn in the peanut butter to make the teeth.

5. Use the other slices to make three more treats.

Your friends will gobble them up!

SILLY HALLOWEEN STORY

Write a silly story by filling in the blanks.

I have a problem. A really, really,

_____ problem. I don't know
      an adjective

what to be for _____. My
          a holiday

friend _____ thinks I should
        a friend

be a _____. My other friend
      noun

_____ thinks I should be a
    a friend

_____. Maybe I should be
    noun

a _____ _____.
     adjective   noun

They are really _____
                        adjective

and _____. My
              adjective

_____ _____
     adjective   family member

says I need to decide soon. _____
                                    holiday

is only _____ days away! I have
              a number

to _____ soon before it's too late.
        verb

Please _____ me, so I can have a
              verb

_____ and _____
     adjective   adjective

_____.
     holiday

Have you read all about Freddy?

Don't miss any of Freddy's funny adventures!

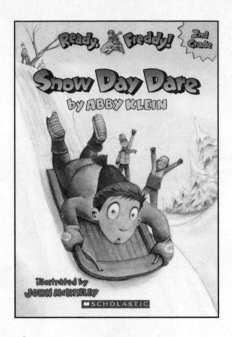

Time to go sledding!

It's snowing, which means snowball fights, forts—and a snow day break from school! If only the biggest bully in second grade, Max, hadn't dared Freddy to sled down Cherry Hill. That hill is so steep and scary, Freddy's never taken his sled to the top . . . but maybe with the help of his friends, this could be the best snow day ever!